The Best Dog in the World

Elliot walked home deep in thought. Someone would be bound to adopt Denzil – but then he'd never see him again. And the alternative didn't bear thinking about. He knew it would only be a last resort because Nick and Angela really cared about the dogs.

If only there was a way he could adopt Denzil…

Look out for more books by Sylvia Green!

Christmas Quackers
The Softhearted Sheepdog
The Best Christmas Ever
The Christmas Pony
A Parsnip Called Val
The Christmas Wish

Sylvia Green

The Best
Dog in the World

Illustrated by Sophie Keen

SCHOLASTIC

For Alex Bradley Ford

Scholastic Children's Books,
Euston House, 24 Eversholt Street,
London NW1 1DB, UK
a division of Scholastic Ltd
London ~ New York ~ Toronto ~ Sydney ~ Auckland
Mexico City ~ New Delhi ~ Hong Kong

First published in the UK by Scholastic Ltd, 2005

10 digit ISBN 0 439 96064 9
13 digit ISBN 978 0439 96064 9
10 digit Fairs edition ISBN 0 439 95457 6
13 digit Fairs edition ISBN 978 0439 95457 0

Printed and bound by Nørhaven Paperback A/S, Denmark

2 4 6 8 10 9 7 5 3

Chapter 1

Elliot
The Dogs' Home

Elliot turned the corner and there was the dogs' home. He quickened his pace. "I don't know why I didn't think of this months ago," he said to himself. "As soon as Mum ruined all my hopes of having a pet. Why on earth did she have to go and marry boring old Myles?"

He felt a bit guilty as soon as he'd said it. Myles was always nice to him.

"But he is boring and she knew I wanted her to marry someone with a nice house and garden in the country," said Elliot.

"Somewhere where I could keep lots of animals."

Myles not only didn't have a house and a garden in the country, he didn't have a house at all. He'd moved into their small flat with them! Their small flat where they weren't allowed to keep any pets.

And the absolute worst thing of all was that Myles was allergic to animals. Anything with fur or feathers made him start sneezing and brought him out in a rash.

Elliot reached the gate and smiled as an assortment of barks greeted him. He instantly pictured the different dogs, the big ones with the deep throaty woofs right down to the small ones with high pitched yaps. He couldn't wait to see them.

There was a bell on the wall with a sign that read: Please ring and Nick or Angela will be with you shortly.

Elliot eagerly pressed the bell.

A tall man appeared straight away. "Hello there," he said. "What can I do for you?"

Elliot guessed it was Nick. "Hi, I'm Elliot. I've come to help you with the dogs."

Nick smiled at him. "Well, Elliot, that's very kind of you, but I'm afraid children aren't allowed to help with the dogs."

Elliot's face fell.

"But I really love animals – especially dogs – and I just want to spend some time with them. I live close by and I don't mind what I do."

"Maybe your mum or your dad could adopt you a dog from here," suggested Nick. "There are lots that need a good home and—"

"They can't," Elliot interrupted him. "I haven't got a real dad – just Mum – and Myles." Then he told him about Myles and his allergy and the flats where they lived.

Nick looked sorry for him. "Look, I can spare ten minutes, how about if I take you to meet one or two of the dogs? At least you can have a chat with them."

Elliot brightened up. "Perhaps I can cheer them up a bit."

"Sure," said Nick, opening the gate. "We do our best for them but we're always so busy, we don't get time to give them as much individual attention as we'd like."

As Elliot followed Nick over to the runs, all the dogs started barking and jumping up at the wire. "They do this every time someone comes in," said Nick. "They're hoping you've come to adopt them."

He introduced him to Sam, a lively Labrador, whose elderly owner could no longer cope with him. Then to Flash, a greyhound that had been retired from racing. Opposite them was Bella, a sleek black poodle who had one blue eye and one yellow eye.

"Bella's owners bred her for a show dog," Nick explained. "But with two different coloured eyes she wouldn't win any prizes so they didn't want to keep her."

"That's awful," said Elliot. "Fancy getting rid of her because of that."

"At least they brought her in here and didn't just dump her, the way some people do," said Nick. "And I'm afraid we also get animals that have been ill-treated or neglected. There are some strange people around."

Elliot wanted a dog so badly, he found it hard to believe people could be like that.

"And this —" said Nick, pointing to a

bundle of matted, brown fur lying in the next run – "is Denzil. He's a stray – been living rough for some time by the looks of him. The dog warden picked him up hanging round the back of McDonald's."

Elliot peered into the run. It looked just like a heap of dog hair that someone had swept up but then he saw it was moving gently as the animal breathed. He stared at the tangled mass and could just pick out a long shaggy ear and then a longer furry mass at the other end that had to be his tail.

Then he noticed his feet – big, hairy, ungainly feet. Denzil was the scruffiest dog he'd ever seen.

Chapter 2

Denzil
King of the Road

Denzil was dreaming of hamburgers. He could hear all the other dogs barking. They were obviously jealous of his HUGE hamburger. He could almost taste it…

"Hello, Denzil."

The voice interrupted his dream – just as he was about to take a bite. He opened one eye and peered through his tangled mass of hair. A boy was standing there looking at him.

"Hey, you're a great dog," said the boy.

Great? thought Denzil. *Me?* No one had

ever said that to him. It was usually a case of "Look at the state of that one" before they moved on to look at the other dogs – the ones that actually wanted to be adopted. The ones that were jumping up at the wire and barking right now. *Some dogs*, thought Denzil, *just have no pride*.

Denzil couldn't understand a dog wanting to be owned by anyone. A free spirit, that was him. King of the road – his own boss. He went where he liked, when he liked. *All right, so I've been picked up at the moment*, he admitted to himself. *But I'll be on my way again very soon*.

"I'm Elliot," said the boy.

Denzil opened his other eye. *Why's he telling me his name? I hope he doesn't expect me to shake paws or anything*. Denzil wasn't into doing tricks for humans.

"Can I stroke him?" asked Elliot.

The boy was with Nick. Nick was OK, and so was his wife, Angela. They treated him pretty well and the food was quite good here too.

Denzil was an expert on dogs' homes; he'd been picked up and put in several over the years. But he always managed to escape – after he'd had a few good meals.

"OK, you can stroke him," said Nick, unbolting the door. "He's actually very docile, for a stray."

Docile? thought Denzil. *Of course I'm docile. Just because I'm a dog of the road* (he hated the word stray) *doesn't mean I'm going to savage everyone!* His mother had been a dog of the road too and she'd been very proud of the fact. She'd taught Denzil a lot about life, and he'd gone on to learn more himself over the years. Denzil was a pretty streetwise dog by now. He knew what was what.

Nick brought the boy into his run. He kept perfectly still as Elliot bent down and gently stroked him on his head and over his long shaggy ears. Only his eyes moved as he watched for any sudden movement. He didn't trust humans.

Elliot stroked him all the way down his back to the long tangled mass that was his tail. "He's such a great dog," he said.

Nick chuckled. "Why do you like this one so much?"

"I don't know," said Elliot. "He's different – kind of special."

Special? Denzil had been called a lot of things in his life, but never special.

Then Elliot picked up an old rubber ball that was lying next to him. "Come on, Denzil," he said, rolling it across the run. "Fetch it, boy. Fetch the ball."

You kidding? thought Denzil. *I don't do "fetch". Why should I? I don't want the ball – and if he wants it, he can fetch it himself.*

"I don't think he's used to playing," said Nick. "And I'm sorry, but I've got to get back to work so you'll have to go home now."

Elliot looked disappointed. "OK. But can

I come and see him again?"

Nick chuckled. "All right. As long as Angela or myself are around."

Denzil watched Nick bolt the door behind them. *Why does Elliot want to see me again?* he wondered.

As soon as they'd gone, Bella, the poodle in the next run came over to the wire. "So you've finally clicked then," she snapped. "Course, the poor boy must be short-sighted. Must have forgotten his glasses."

"What are you talking about?" asked Denzil, sitting up for a good scratch.

"Don't listen to her," said Flash, the greyhound. "She's just jealous that the boy wants to adopt you and not her."

"Adopt me?" Denzil jumped to his feet. "I don't want to be adopted. Not by anyone."

"Why not?" asked Sam, the Labrador. "Every dog wants a nice comfortable home with kind people to look after them."

"Not me," said Denzil. "I'll be escaping

from here – and soon. I've got places to go, new smells to sniff. I'm a free spirit." He'd heard about living with humans – there were responsibilities attached. You had to chew slippers and chase the postman. And for some reason they kept throwing things like balls and sticks and then expecting you to fetch them back.

He gave himself a good shake and bits of fur flew everywhere.

"Ugh, you're disgusting," said Bella, jumping back, her blue and yellow eyes flashing. "The sooner I get adopted the better. I'm bound to get a really good home, my previous owners were heartbroken when they had to give me up."

Denzil didn't answer her. If that was what she wanted to believe, that was up to her. But he'd seen it all before – dogs bought or bred as show dogs, then if there was something even slightly wrong with them, they were got rid of.

That was humans for you.

Then there was Flash. He'd been a really good racing greyhound, won lots of races for his owner. But now he was too old to race...

"What sort of dog are you anyway?" asked Bella.

"Me? I'm a Bitsa," said Denzil.

"I've never heard of a Bitsa," said Sam.

"It means I'm bitsa this breed and bitsa that breed," said Denzil. "I've got a bit of Irish Wolfhound in me, a bit of Old English Sheepdog, some Labrador, bloodhound..." He paused and looked at Bella. "I don't think I've got any poodle."

Bella looked at him haughtily. "Definitely not," she said.

They were interrupted by Angela opening Denzil's run. "Come on, Denzil, let's give you a bath to spruce you up a bit."

Denzil sighed. It was the same, every time he got picked up – they always wanted to give him a bath. But the truth of the matter was, he never looked any different!

Chapter 3

Elliot
If only...

Elliot went back to the dogs' home the very next day. He met Abbie and Kai McFarlane, who were in his class at school, just coming out with their father. He felt a pang of jealously as he saw they had Sam the Labrador on a lead.

"Hi, Elliot," said Abbie. "We've just adopted Sam."

"Isn't he great?" said Kai. "Have you come to adopt a dog too?"

"No." Elliot stooped to make a fuss of Sam. "I'm not allowed to."

He watched them leave, Sam's tail wagging enthusiastically. Then Nick told him that Angela was cleaning out the runs, so he could go and chat to Denzil while she was there.

Elliot went straight over. Angela had finished cleaning Denzil's run and was just letting him out of his kennel. The dog ambled out into his run and looked up at Elliot. Elliot thought he looked a bit surprised.

"Hi, Denzil. I bet you didn't expect to see me again so soon, did you?"

Angela smiled at Elliot. "Come to keep Denzil company, have you? Nick told me how much you like him."

Elliot nodded.

"I gave him a bath yesterday," said Angela, as she started hosing down Bella's run. "But he doesn't look any different."

Elliot smiled at the scruffy dog. "He looks great, just as he is."

He intended to visit Denzil as often as he could – as long as he was there – as long as someone hadn't adopted him, or…

"What happens to dogs that no one adopts?" he asked Angela.

"Well, we try to re-home them for as long as possible," she told him. "We don't like to give up, but space is limited especially now, just after Christmas. It's a very busy time of year. Some people buy dogs for Christmas presents then either the puppy grows bigger than they expected or they just get fed up with looking after them."

"That's awful," said Elliot. "I'd never get fed up, or worry about how big they got – if I had a dog."

Angela smiled at him. "Puppies are quite easy to find new homes for, but not all dogs are suitable for re-homing. You get the odd vicious one and then there's the strays. Long-term strays are not usually house-trained – which tends to put people off – and they don't always bond with humans."

"Is Denzil what you'd call a long-term stray?" asked Elliot.

"Well, yes, he is," said Angela. "But like I said, we don't like to give up."

"But what if you do have to give up?" Elliot persisted. He felt he just had to know.

"Well, only if we're full up and we need the space," Angela began slowly. "And only if they've been here a long time and we really don't think there's any hope of them being adopted. Well, we have to take them to the vet…"

She didn't finish. She didn't have to. Elliot shut his eyes to keep out the dreadful image. That wasn't going to happen to Denzil – it just couldn't.

"Hey, cheer up," said Angela. "There are lots of really kind people around. Maybe someone will want to take Denzil on."

Elliot smiled at her. Then he turned back to Denzil and took a red ball out of his pocket. "Here, Denzil, I've brought you a new ball as you didn't seem to like the one you've got." Denzil really seemed to be listening to him this time. He was watching him with his beautiful black eyes – at least, what Elliot could see of them through the dog's tangled hair. "It's really my ball," Elliot told him. "But you can have it."

He tossed it over the wire into the run but Denzil ignored it as it bounced around him. "Oh well, I expect you'll play with it later when I've gone," said Elliot.

He stayed talking to Denzil until Angela had finished cleaning the runs.

Elliot walked home deep in thought. Someone would be bound to adopt Denzil – but then he'd never see him again. And the alternative didn't bear thinking about. He knew it would only be a last resort because Nick and Angela really cared about the dogs.

If only there was a way he could adopt Denzil.

The lift was broken again so he climbed the eighty-eight steps up to their flat. He wanted to talk to Mum about Denzil but she was resting. She'd just given up her job as a nurse because she was expecting a baby soon – hers and Myles's baby. A sudden image of a frilly baby's bonnet flashed into Elliot's mind. Peeping out of the bonnet was a tiny Myles face complete with glasses.

Myles was putting up a shelf, for yet more of his books. He had loads of them and he even worked in a bookshop. He spent loads of time reading and never played any sports or anything. Elliot supposed it was something to do with him being old – he was almost forty! Several years older than Elliot's mum.

On the table was a book on bringing up babies and another one on babies' names. A third book was open at the page showing how to put up a shelf.

Myles was really enthusiastic about his shelf. "Tell you what, Elliot. You can help me, if you like," he said.

Elliot sighed and passed him the screwdriver but his mind wasn't on the job. It was back at the dogs' home with Denzil. He was going to visit him as often as he could – as long as he was still there – and he was going take him lots of treats.

Chapter 4

Denzil

"They're not getting a lead on me!"

A week later Denzil was still at the home. He'd never stayed in one so long. He slumped down on the floor of his run – but immediately jumped up again as a high-pitched squeak came from under him.

He looked down crossly at the stupid bone-shaped bit of rubber. *Why on earth would Elliot think I wanted an imitation bone that squeaks?* he wondered for probably the fiftieth time. Then he looked at the rubber chicken, the large stick and the bright red ball. Elliot kept bringing him things, and he'd been back every day the past week.

"So why haven't you escaped yet?" Bella interrupted his thoughts. "What's keeping you?" The proud black poodle was in a bad mood. She'd really thought a couple were going to adopt her that morning and then, at the last moment, they'd chosen a little brown and white spaniel instead. She was sure it was just because both the spaniel's eyes were the same colour, unlike hers.

"I'll be back on the road any day now," said Denzil.

"It's that boy, isn't it?" snapped Bella. "All your talk about being a 'dog of the road' and not wanting to be adopted. You're no different to the rest of us."

Denzil shook himself irritably. "I've told you, I don't want to be adopted," he barked. "I'll go when it suits me – it's nothing to do with the boy."

"He has been back several times," Flash pointed out. "And he never looks at any of the other dogs – it's just you he's interested in."

"He stays for ages," said Bella. "And brings you presents."

"What do I want presents for?" Denzil turned tail on her and went to lie down at the back of his run. The truth was, he didn't really know himself why he hadn't escaped yet. He only usually stayed in a rescue home long enough to have a couple of good meals and then he was off. Back on the open road where he belonged. There'd never been a home he couldn't escape from yet and he'd already worked out how to slide the bolt on this door by watching Nick and Angela.

So why was he still here? Denzil didn't really understand it himself, he was usually itching to get away. It couldn't be anything to do with Elliot – he didn't need anyone. The nearest Denzil had ever got to having a friend was Harvey, the soft-hearted sheepdog, who he'd met in one of the homes. Harvey now lived on a turkey farm and Denzil visited him sometimes. He'd been invited to stay but he'd never even been tempted.

Denzil made a decision. He'd go tomorrow, after breakfast, and then maybe he'd find the remains of a hamburger for dinner. He licked his lips. He hadn't had a good hamburger for ages.

"Hey, Denzil. I'm back." It was Elliot. Denzil found himself getting up to greet him. Well, it was the least he could do as he was leaving tomorrow.

"Look what I've brought you today," said Elliot, holding out a bag. "Super Whopper Doggy Chocs."

Super what? thought Denzil. *What on earth am I supposed to do with them?*

Elliot opened the bag and took out a couple of large, round, brown shapes. He pushed them through the wire. "I bought them with my pocket money."

Denzil sniffed them. They smelt nice. He'd smelt something similar once before when a little girl had dropped something she was eating in the park. Her mother hadn't let her pick it up again but Denzil had been happy to pick it up – and eat it!

Denzil quickly ate up all the Super Whopper Doggy Chocs. This was the kind of present he liked.

"Guess what?" said Elliot. "Nick says I can take you for a walk today. He's going to give Flash some exercise so he says I can go with him and take you as well."

A walk? thought Denzil. *Oh no, that's going too far. I don't need anyone to take me for a walk.*

"I've got a lead for you here," said Elliot, whipping it out of his pocket. "Nick's going to put it on you for me."

Oh no, he's not, thought Denzil. *I'm king of the open road – a free spirit. They're not getting a lead on me.*

Nick arrived and slid the bolt on the door and he and Elliot came into the run. Denzil shrank back against the wall of his kennel.

"Oh come on, Denzil," said Elliot, bending down to him. "It'll be fun."

Denzil looked up at him. Elliot had brought him Super Whopper Doggy Chocs and he had said he was a great dog. No one had ever said that about him before. A mangy mutt, he'd been called only recently when he was helping himself to a burnt sausage out of a man's dustbin. Why the man had been so protective about a burnt sausage he couldn't imagine. He'd obviously thrown it away in the first place! Denzil would never understand humans.

"Please, Denzil," said Elliot.

Denzil looked into his eyes. There was something there – a sadness – but a kind of longing too. He slowly came forward. *I suppose it won't do any harm*, he thought. *And it is for Elliot's sake – the boy has been kind to me.*

He allowed Nick to put the collar and lead on him. He didn't like the collar, it was uncomfortable and felt itchy. He only ever wore one when he'd been picked up by the dog warden.

Nick gave the lead to Elliot and went to get Flash, then the four of them walked towards the big field. Denzil pretended to let Elliot lead him and padded along beside him on his over-large paws. He knew he was walking on his own but if Elliot wanted to think he was leading him, then it was OK.

Wait a minute, he thought. *What am I doing? I've never wanted to please a human before.*

Chapter 5

Elliot
"I wish you really were my dog."

Elliot happily led Denzil round the field. He'd met Abbie and Kai, walking Sam, on his way to the home. Now it was his turn. He was pretending that Denzil really was his dog and he was just taking him for his daily walk.

Nick was being pulled ahead by Flash, who was obviously used to going a lot faster.

Elliot decided to run too. "Come on, boy," he called to Denzil, tugging gently at his lead.

Denzil resisted a bit at first but then he began to run alongside Elliot. After a while he started to bound ahead and Elliot had to run faster to keep up with him. Round and round the field they went, the dog's large paws pounding the ground and his long shaggy ears bouncing up and down. They overtook Nick and Flash not just once, but twice.

Elliot laughed out loud as the wind blew in his hair. "Wow, you can really go, Denzil," he called. "Oh, this is just great!"

All too soon it was time for Denzil to go back in his run. Elliot was quite out of breath and his face was glowing in the cold air as he said goodbye.

He ruffled Denzil's shaggy coat. "Oh, Denzil, I wish, I wish, I wish that you really were my dog. I wish, I really wish that I could take you home with me."

Denzil stared up at him, panting, his long tongue hanging out. His tangled hair was swept back from his face and Elliot thought that his black eyes looked puzzled. "Don't worry, Denzil, I'll be back soon," Elliot told him. "You're just the best dog in the whole world."

Elliot was thoughtful as he walked home. Every time he went to the home he was relieved to find Denzil was still there. He was pleased no one had adopted him, although he couldn't understand why – even though he was a long-term stray. He was easily the best dog there.

But several more dogs had been taken into the home that week and it was actually full. In fact Sam's old run now had two smaller dogs in it. They were running short of space and Denzil couldn't stay there for ever…

"Nick and Angela know how much I love him," he reassured himself. "Surely they won't let anything happen… Oh, if only I could find a way to keep him myself."

Mum was waiting for him when he arrived home. "Myles has got a surprise for you," she told him. "He's in your room."

Elliot quickly went into his bedroom. Myles was in there putting up a shelf. He gave Elliot a beaming smile.

"This is for your books," he told him. "And in particular, your book – on goldfish."

"But, I haven't got…" Elliot started. Then he saw the book with a large orange goldfish on the cover lying on his bed. "OK, I have got a book on goldfish," he said. "You've bought me one. But why?"

He stopped as his eyes followed to where Myles was pointing. On his chest of drawers was a bowl with two goldfish in. They had a little bridge to swim under and some dark green water weed planted in the multi-coloured gravel at the bottom.

"I know how much you want a pet," said Myles. "And I'm not allergic to fish, so I bought them for you."

"Well – er – thanks," said Elliot. "But we're not allowed to keep *any* pets in the flats."

"Oh, I don't think anyone will complain about a couple of fish," he said. "After all they're not going to make much noise, are they?" Myles laughed and then mum came in and laughed too. She always thought Myles's jokes were hilarious.

"Wasn't it kind of Myles?" she said.

"Yes, it was," said Elliot. And it was kind of him – it was just that… Then Elliot spotted the cot folded up behind the door. "Why's that in here?"

"Well, the baby will be sharing your room," said Mum. "We've only got two bedrooms and you've got plenty of space in here."

"I'm going to fix it up really nice for the two of you," said Myles. "It'll be fun for you to have someone to share with – apart from the fish, of course." He laughed again and Mum joined in.

Elliot had a quick vision of the baby in the frilly bonnet that looked just like Myles again. Only this time it was sitting on the shelf in his room reading a book!

He watched the illegal fish swimming round in their bowl. They were nice, but he didn't want to share his room with the new baby. He wouldn't mind sharing it with Denzil though.

Chapter 6

Denzil
A Ginormous Decision

Denzil was worried. Two days had now passed since he'd decided to escape from the home – but he was still there.

What's up with me? he thought. *It's not that I can't escape.* He'd even got as far as sliding the bolt on the door last night but somehow he couldn't bring himself to actually go.

He kept thinking about when Elliot was coming again.

At least Bella had stopped getting at him – a little girl and her mum had decided to adopt her. The little girl thought that

43

Bella's different coloured eyes were "really sweet" and they were picking her up that afternoon. That was one happy poodle.

Flash had been taken to somewhere called Greyhound Rescue where he could live happily with other greyhounds. Several other dogs had been re-homed but more had come in. A couple of times he'd caught Nick looking at him and saying to Angela, "I don't know what we're going to do about Denzil." Well, they didn't have to do anything about him – he was his own boss – a free spirit. He'd sort himself out, as he always had.

Denzil lay down in his run and put his paws over his ears to shut out the noise of the other dogs barking. "I must be mad staying here. Especially as Elliot only comes for a little while each day." He sat straight up again. He'd finally admitted it. He was staying just so he could see Elliot. It was quite a shock to him.

Elliot arrived in the afternoon. Denzil immediately jumped up and wagged his shaggy tail in greeting.

"I bet you thought I wasn't coming, didn't you?" said Elliot. "Well, Myles decided to cook the lunch, as it's Saturday. He's bought this cook book on healthy eating and he decided to make his own hamburgers. It took ages."

Denzil's ears pricked up. They had hamburgers at their house!

Nick came and put Denzil's lead on and Elliot was allowed to walk him round the field on his own. They walked and ran together and jumped over logs and all the time Elliot talked to him and laughed.

Denzil was baffled. *Why is this so much fun?* he wondered. He'd never been one for running about unless it was necessary – like when he was being chased off by someone. *But it is fun*, he thought. He'd never felt so happy. *It must be – it can only be – Elliot.*

It was after Nick had put him back in his run and Elliot was saying goodbye that Denzil made his decision. A ginormous, momentous, decision. He wanted to be with Elliot – always. He even wanted Elliot to take him home with him. (And it wasn't just because they had hamburgers at their house.) He actually wanted to be adopted!

I can't believe it, he thought. *Me, Denzil, king of the road, free spirit, I want to be adopted – by Elliot.*

All he had to do was let him know. *Elliot's always saying he wishes he could take me home with him*, he thought. *Well now he can.*

Denzil knew what to do. He'd seen the other dogs do it often enough. He started jumping up at the wire and barking. He felt a bit self-conscious at first but he had to let Elliot know that he wanted him to adopt him.

Elliot laughed. "It's all right, Denzil, I'll be back tomorrow."

He wasn't getting the message.

I'll have to try the soulful eyes, thought Denzil. *That never fails. Gets 'em every time.*

Denzil had never lowered himself to anything like this before but he managed the most beautiful soulful eyes as he looked pleadingly up at Elliot.

That certainly moved him. Elliot had tears in his eyes as he crouched down to speak to him.

"Hey, Denzil. You're the greatest dog in the world, you know that? And I really wish I could take you home with me, but I'm not allowed."

Then he was gone, leaving Denzil completely baffled.

The little girl and the lady arrived to collect Bella. The poodle paused as she was led past Denzil. There was concern in her blue and yellow eyes. "I'm sorry, Denzil. I really thought he wanted to adopt you. You'll find someone else, you'll see."

But Denzil didn't see. He didn't just want to be adopted – he wanted to be with Elliot. Why wasn't he allowed to take him?

"I've got it," he said. "He's not allowed to adopt me because he's too small. Whenever someone comes to collect a dog – like that little girl who's just taken Bella – they have a big person with them. Grown-ups, they're called."

The more he thought about it, the more sure he was. Elliot always came on his own. Maybe his grown-up couldn't come. Or maybe he didn't have one. Poor Elliot.

There was only one thing for it – he'd have to take matters into his own paws.

Denzil jumped up and, pushing his nose up against the wire, managed to grasp the bolt with his teeth. A quick, expert flick of his head and the door swung open.

Then he was off, wind blowing through his fur as he raced after Elliot, following his scent. *Good job I've got a bit of bloodhound in me*, he thought.

Chapter 7

Elliot
"What am I going to do with you?"

Elliot turned round in surprise as he heard a bark. The next minute he was hit by a flurry of tangled fur jumping up at him.

"Denzil! What, are you doing here?" He knew Nick had bolted the door, he'd seen him do it. "How did you get out?"

A long pink tongue started licking his face.

Elliot laughed and wiped his wet face with his sleeve. "It's great that you're so pleased to see me but you can't stay out here – I'll have to take you back."

Denzil immediately jumped away from him and barked.

"What's the matter, boy? Don't you like the home?"

Denzil barked again and backed away.

"I suppose you can't want to be in the home or you wouldn't have escaped," said Elliot. "But what am I going to do with you?"

Denzil crept forward again. "I can't just leave you loose – you might get injured. Plus you might get lost and then I'll never see you again."

Denzil looked up at him, his head cocked to one side. He looked puzzled.

Elliot ruffled his fur. "And I can't take you home with me."

He looked into the dog's eyes and could see he was hurt, very hurt. Elliot couldn't bear it. Denzil had obviously escaped to be with him. What was he going to do?

"I know." He had a sudden idea. "I could take you to Abbie and Kai's. They adopted

Sam, remember? They love dogs and I'm sure one more won't make any difference – and I'll even be able to come and visit you there."

Denzil still looked puzzled but he trotted alongside Elliot as he walked to the twins' house.

Sam's barking greeted them from the other side of the door when Elliot knocked.

The twins' mother opened it holding on to Sam's collar.

"Hello, Mrs McFarlane," Elliot started.

But she wasn't looking at him – she was looking at Denzil. "What's that?" she exclaimed.

"It's a dog," Elliot told her indignantly. "He's called Denzil."

"It looks more like a filthy old floor mop with legs," said Mrs McFarlane.

Elliot bent down and covered Denzil's ears. "Please don't say that, you'll hurt his feelings. He needs a home – at least, for now."

"Well he's not coming in my house," said Mrs McFarlane, struggling to hold Sam back. "This one is quite enough to look after." She closed the door.

It opened again immediately and Abbie and Kai were there. Sam shot out to greet Denzil and the two dogs happily went off to investigate the front garden.

"We heard what happened," said Kai.

"I suppose you're not allowed to keep animals in your flats," said Abbie.

"No," said Elliot. "Although Mrs Phipps has a secret cat which only goes out on her balcony and Mr Barns has a budgie. And now I've got two goldfish, but it's not just that." He told her about Myles and his allergy.

"Our dad says he's allergic to grass seed," said Abbie. "But Mum says it's all in his mind – he just doesn't want to do the gardening."

Elliot was thoughtful. "D'you think it can

be just in the mind? D'you think maybe Myles isn't really allergic to animals – he just thinks he is?"

"Could be," said Abbie. "Have you ever seen him with an animal?"

"No I haven't, he just said that he comes out in a rash and starts sneezing every time he gets near anything with fur or feathers."

"Well, you could always test him out," said Kai. "Get Denzil near to him without him knowing."

"I could, couldn't I?" said Elliot.

He remembered that Mum and Myles were going shopping for a pram and other baby things that afternoon so they'd probably still be out. All he had to do was smuggle Denzil into his room. He'd have to keep him hidden, with animals not being allowed in the flats. But with Mrs Phipps's secret cat, Mr Barns's budgie and his illegal goldfish, what difference would one more creature make?

He made the decision.

"Come on, Denzil," he called. "I'm taking you home."

Denzil happily bounded alongside him as they raced over to Elliot's flats.

Amazingly, no one seemed to be around. Denzil was a bit reluctant to go inside the building but Elliot eventually persuaded him to climb the stairs. (He knew he wouldn't like the lift, even though it was working now.) Elliot opened the door to his flat and led Denzil into the living room.

"I'll have to keep you hidden in my room for now," he told him. "I'll sneak you out for a walk later when they're watching TV. Then tomorrow I'll let you out and Myles will be so surprised that you've been here all evening and night. I bet he'll be really pleased to find he isn't allergic after all."

Denzil immediately started sniffing round the furniture. Elliot smiled as he watched him.

"D'you like it here, Denzil?" Then the scruffy dog sat down on the carpet and had a good scratch.

"No, come on, boy, you've got to go in my room."

Denzil stood up and shook himself, fur was flying everywhere. "Oh no," cried Elliot. "I'll have to get this all cleared up before they get back."

He managed to get Denzil into his room and had just shut the door behind him when Mum and Myles came in.

Elliot watched in horror as wisps of fur wafted across the room towards them.

Myles sniffed a couple of times then he started sneezing. His eyes streamed and his face rapidly turned all red and blotchy.

Chapter 8

Denzil
"He's not even house-trained!"

Denzil was startled by all the noise coming from the other room. And in any case he was beginning to feel claustrophobic – he'd never been inside a house before and he hated being shut in.

He barked and jumped up at the door. It flew open and he bounded out.

A lady with a big tummy screamed and a strange man with a red blotchy face was sneezing all over the place. Elliot was crying and saying he was sorry. Whatever could he have done?

Elliot wouldn't have done anything wrong, so Denzil started barking again to tell them.

"For goodness sake, get him out of here," shouted the lady with the big tummy. "I'll have to thoroughly clean the whole flat now."

It looked all right to Denzil.

"And look," she screamed, pointing to the bedroom doorway. "He's not even house-trained!" Denzil saw Elliot's mouth drop open as he looked at the offending pile on the bedroom carpet.

What's wrong with that? thought Denzil. *Doesn't everyone do it?*

Elliot wiped his eyes on his sleeve and bent down to Denzil gently tugging at the tangled fur on the back of his neck. "Come on, boy."

He led him past the sneezing man whose face had turned almost purple now, right to the tips of his ears.

"And come straight back," called the lady, as they went out of the door.

Make your mind up, thought Denzil. *You just told him to go.*

Humans were always strange but those two seemed stranger than usual. Elliot led him down the stairs. He was different, he was OK and Denzil was happy just to be with him. *I wonder where we're going next?* he thought.

Out in the street, it had started to snow. Elliot bent down to Denzil. "I'm really sorry," he told him. "But I can't think of anywhere else you can go. I'll have to take you back to the home."

Denzil immediately pulled away from him. He looked up at Elliot. *Did he say, take me back to the home?*

"Oh, come on, Denzil," Elliot pleaded. "I can't just leave you wandering round the streets. You'll have to go back."

Oh no I won't. Denzil turned tail on him and ran. He ran till he was sure Elliot had stopped following him, then he slowed down to a trot.

A large tabby cat came round the corner.

"Hey, Denzil," said the cat. "Haven't seen you around for a while."

"I've been away," Denzil growled softly. "But I'm back now – for good."

As the cat went on its way, Denzil spotted a hamburger carton lying in the gutter. But he didn't even bother to investigate it, he'd completely lost his appetite. He flopped down behind an old building.

He'd never felt so hurt. This was the first time in his whole life that he'd trusted anyone. The first time he'd decided that he wanted to be with someone and he – Elliot – didn't want him. It was just as he'd always thought, humans weren't to be trusted – not any of them – not even Elliot!

Denzil lay down with his head on his paws, snowflakes gently covering him. *I've learned my lesson – I'll never, ever be fooled again. I'll go back to how I've always been, on my own, trusting no one.*

Chapter 9

Elliot
"Oh, where are you, Denzil?"

Elliot searched for Denzil all day on Sunday but there was no sign of him anywhere. He had wanted to search for him the previous night too, but his mum hadn't let him. He hardly noticed the snow which had been falling lightly all day. He had to find the dog soon – before he got too far away.

Mum had told him firmly to give up all thoughts of having a dog. "And you're not to have anything more to do with Denzil," she insisted. "You've got to get used to the idea."

But Elliot couldn't give up on Denzil – he had to find him. At least the twins were sympathetic. He bumped into them while he was out searching and they offered to help. That was great – three pairs of eyes had much more chance of spotting the missing dog. Plus it also meant he'd be able to search further afield as Mum didn't like him going far on his own.

"But what will you do with Denzil if we do find him?" asked Kai.

"I don't know," said Elliot, "but I've got to make sure he's all right. And I've got to try and explain to him – he thinks I don't care."

They searched before and after school all the following week. Sometimes, after school, they took Sam along too – hoping he could help to find Denzil. Elliot just told Mum he was with the twins – which, of course, wasn't actually a lie.

It was much colder now and there had

been quite a lot more snow, but the three children just trudged through it calling to the missing dog. They searched everywhere they could think of, asked everyone they met but there was no sign of Denzil anywhere. Elliot even checked back at the dogs' home and Angela promised to let him know if the dog wardens picked him up again.

Myles was trying to be nice to him. When Elliot got home on Friday evening he told him he'd got a surprise for him. "I've had the day off work today and I've been very busy."

Elliot spotted the book on the table. *Decorating Made Easy.*

"I've been re-decorating your bedroom and I've stencilled animals all over the walls," he told Elliot. "There's lions, tigers, elephants, kangaroos and bears," he said. "And lots of dogs, of course."

Elliot managed a half-smile. "That's kind of you," he said. At least Myles was trying. He opened the bedroom door. Myles

66

obviously couldn't help being allergic to animals it was just…

He stopped in horror. The animals were all bright pinks, blues, reds, yellows and greens. It looked awful! Why couldn't Myles ever get anything right?

"I thought the bright colours would appeal to the baby too," said Myles cheerfully.

Elliot had been finding it difficult to sleep all week, but when he did get to sleep that night he dreamed he was being chased by a bright-red elephant and a green kangaroo with yellow spots.

He was pleased the next day was Saturday, he had the whole day to search for Denzil. He had no luck in the morning and in the afternoon the twins joined him along with Sam, who was straining at his lead, eager to be off.

"Where shall we look today?" asked Abbie. "We've searched just about the whole town now."

"I'm just looking everywhere again," said Elliot. "Denzil won't have stayed in one place and anyway we might have missed him."

It was snowing quite hard as they trudged the streets, calling to Denzil. They searched down alleyways, under hedges and round the back of shops.

They'd reached the other side of town when suddenly two older boys rushed past them. They were sliding on the snow and, as they slid past an old lady, they knocked her bags of shopping out of her hands. They ran off laughing, leaving the old lady with her shopping scattered all over the pavement.

Elliot, Abbie and Kai ran up to her. "Are you all right?" asked Abbie.

"Just a bit shaken," she said, but she looked very upset.

Abbie and Elliot started picking up her shopping for her while Kai held on to Sam who was keen to run after the boys.

The old lady only lived a couple of roads away so they helped her back home with the shopping.

"That's so kind of you, dears," she said, sinking into a chair in her kitchen.

Sam slumped down at her feet so Kai started putting the shopping in the cupboard while Abbie made her a cup of tea.

"You will stay and have a cup with me, won't you?" she asked them.

"Of course we will," said Abbie, getting the milk out of the fridge.

Elliot sighed. The old lady was obviously shaken and no doubt lonely too, so how could they refuse? But he wanted to get on with searching for Denzil. Every day that passed meant the dog could be further away, and it would be getting dark very soon.

Oh where are you, Denzil? he thought desperately.

Chapter 10

Denzil
A Secret Dog

Denzil shifted on his sack on the shed floor. "I'll be glad when this snow stops and I can be on my way," he said to himself.

He'd taken refuge from the snow in a very overgrown and neglected garden. He'd been there all week as Hester, the lady who lived there, left him pretty much alone. She'd even given him some scraps a few times and she never tried to get him into the house – or give him a bath!

He got up for a good scratch. "Hester's OK but I'll never trust another human again. They make you think one thing and then they let you down – big time!"

One good thing about staying here was that it was quite near to a hamburger restaurant. Denzil popped out regularly to find leftovers and once someone even chucked one over the garden wall.

He ambled over to the shed doorway to look out. "The king of the road will be off again soon. All those places to see, all those new smells to sniff –" He stopped as he heard Hester's voice.

"The dog's out here," she said. "He doesn't want to come in the house. I bought that tin of dog food for the poor little chap for a treat."

"Where is he? Is he in that shed?"

The voice was familiar. *It's Elliot!* thought Denzil.

Denzil had heard Elliot calling him several times but he'd kept hidden. Now he was here – Hester was bringing him into the garden.

He'd have to hide…

But then Sam was bounding down the garden, barking like mad. He'd spotted him. It was too late.

"Denzil!" Elliot rushed past Sam and threw his arms round him. "Oh, where have you been? I've been looking everywhere for you."

Denzil tried to pull away but Elliot held on to him, hugging him.

Then Elliot pushed the tangled hair back from Denzil's face and looked lovingly into his eyes. "I've been so worried about you. Are you all right?"

He sounds just like he cares about me, thought Denzil. *Perhaps, he really does care. But then why did he...? Oh, I'll never understand humans.*

He saw the two girls that had adopted Sam. They came over and stroked him too, even they looked pleased to see him.

Elliot jumped up to talk to Hester. He sounded very excited. "If Denzil could stay living here with you, I could come twice a day to feed him."

"I'd like that," said Hester. "He's company for me, even though he lives out here, and he doesn't need much looking after. He seems to find most of his own food, hamburgers usually but one day he brought back a whole string of sausages. Goodness knows where he gets it all from."

Elliot laughed. "Oh, this is just great. I'll take him for a walk every day too."

Denzil looked up. *Why does he keep thinking I need taking for a walk? But then, it was fun last time...*

"This could prove to be the perfect arrangement for you," said Abbie.

"Yes, but we'll have to keep it a secret," said Elliot. "Mum and Myles will be furious if they find out I've disobeyed them." He quickly explained to Hester what had happened when he'd taken Denzil home.

"Well you won't be harming anyone with him living here," she said. "And it will be lovely for me to have you visiting. It gets a bit lonely here on my own sometimes."

"So it's great all round," said Kai. "We'll come and visit sometimes too. We can take Denzil and Sam for walks together, it will be nice for them."

"We'll have to keep to this side of town," said Elliot. "I can't risk walking him anywhere near home."

Abbie nodded. "And don't worry, we won't tell anyone about Denzil. He'll be our secret."

Denzil sighed. So he was to be a secret dog. Well, that was OK with him. He had somewhere to live now and it wasn't in a stuffy house, he still had his freedom. He had new friends – and he had Elliot. Being a secret dog sounded just fine to him.

Chapter 11

Elliot
A Close Thing

Elliot had never been so happy. He went to see Denzil every morning, on his way to school and again on the way home. Before he went home every evening, Elliot was careful to thoroughly brush all his clothes to remove the dog hair and to wash his hands.

Mum was pleased to see him smiling again. "I'm glad you've got Abbie and Kai for friends," she told him. "It's doing you good, spending time with them." Elliot knew that what she really meant was it was taking his mind off Denzil. If only she knew!

Elliot bought food for Denzil with his pocket money, although fortunately he didn't need much as he found a lot for himself. One of Elliot's first jobs when he arrived at Hester's in the morning was to clear away the empty hamburger cartons the dog had brought home.

Weekends were the best, taking Denzil for long walks in the park. Abbie and Kai usually came and brought Sam as well.

Hester was happy too and always looked pleased to see them. But all three children were beginning to get worried about her.

"She's not coping very well, is she?" said Kai. "The house hasn't been cleaned properly for ages by the look of it."

"Maybe we could help her," suggested Elliot. "In return for all she's doing for us and for Denzil.

"That's really kind of you," said Hester, when they suggested it. "You don't need to do anything – I love having you here. But if it makes you feel better, well, the place does need a bit of sprucing up."

So on Saturday afternoon they decided to start on the kitchen. Abbie and Kai arrived on their bikes as they didn't have Sam with them. The twins' mum was giving him a bath. They started cleaning the cupboards and the work surfaces.

Elliot concentrated on the cooker and was just standing back to admire his handiwork when he noticed a shelf hanging off the wall. "I could fix that for you," he told Hester. "I've helped my stepfather put up shelves often enough, we put another new one up just last night."

"Not more books?" said Abbie.

Elliot nodded. "A new set of encyclopaedias this time."

He popped home to borrow some of Myles's tools. Mum was fast asleep on the bed and Myles was out so Elliot didn't have to think of an excuse why he wanted them.

Hopefully he could sneak them back later without Myles even knowing.

He'd almost reached Hester's road when, to his horror, he spotted a familiar figure walking towards him.

"Myles! Oh no! What's he doing round here?"

It was too late to turn back – Myles had spotted him. Elliot hastily hid the bag of tools behind him.

"Elliot!" called Myles, hurrying towards him. "Where are you off to?"

"Just visiting a friend," said Elliot quickly. "Abbie and Kai are waiting for me there. What are you doing round here?"

"I'm just looking round my old territory," said Myles. "I used to live in this road when I was a boy."

Elliot's heart sank – he had no idea Myles had lived round here.

"Haven't been back for years," said Myles. "That was the house we lived in, over there."

Elliot looked where Myles was pointing. The house was just round the corner to Hester's road. "Er – it looks nice," he said.

"Yes, it was," said Myles. "Anyway better get back. I left your mum having a rest."

"See you later then," said Elliot. He breathed a huge sigh of relief as Myles turned to go. If he hadn't been back for years until now then the chances were he wouldn't come back again for a long time.

Elliot walked round the corner and Hester opened the door to him. "I've got the tools," he told her.

"And would they be my tools by any chance?" said a voice behind him.

Elliot spun round. "Myles!" He stared at him in horror. "You – you followed me."

"You looked so worried when you saw me I knew you were up to something," said Myles. "And I wondered what you were hiding behind your back."

"I – er…" started Elliot but Myles was

81

looking up at the house. Then he switched to staring at Hester.

"Good heavens," he said. "It can't be – can it? Hester Brannon?"

"Well, yes," said Hester. "But – wait a minute. It's Myles, isn't it?"

Myles grinned and nodded. "I thought you'd gone to New Zealand with the rest of the family," he said.

Elliot was speechless. Myles and Hester knew each other. A thousand thoughts were whizzing round in his head and most of them involved Denzil.

"I changed my mind about New Zealand, pretty much at the last minute," said Hester. "I didn't want to leave England. Didn't Robert write and tell you?"

Myles chuckled. "No, Robert didn't get round to writing. He did say he wasn't much good at it before he left. We've lost touch now." He turned to Elliot. "Hester's son and I grew up together."

"Always round here, he was," Hester joined in. "Right pair of tearaways."

Elliot couldn't imagine Myles as a "tearaway" but he thought it was time he warned Hester who he was. "Myles is my stepfather," he told her.

Hester thought for a minute then gave him a knowing wink – she understood. "Elliot has been helping me," she told Myles. "He and the twins often come to give me a hand."

Good old Hester, thought Elliot. *She might be getting old, but she's pretty quick to pick up on the situation.*

Myles looked back at Elliot. "Why didn't you tell us? It's wonderful that you're helping Hester. There was no need to keep it a secret."

"Well – er I don't know really," said Elliot. He could feel himself going red in the face. "I'm sorry I took your tools without asking you but I wanted to fix Hester's kitchen shelf."

"Oh, I'll do that for you," said Myles,

stepping into the hall. "The kitchen's this way, if I remember rightly."

Elliot nervously followed him along the hall to the kitchen. If Denzil stayed in his shed Myles shouldn't be able to see him through the window.

Myles looked at the shelf. "This won't take long."

Elliot passed him his tools and then looked over at Kai who was obviously holding her breath as she watched Myles. Elliot tilted his head towards the garden and mouthed the word *Denzil* to her.

She nodded to him and slipped outside to keep Denzil out of sight.

Myles was getting quite good at shelves now and the job didn't take long, even though he was chatting to Hester about "the old days" all the time.

"It's very kind of you, Myles," said Hester. "And it is good to see you again – just wait till I tell Robert next time he phones."

"Do give him my best," said Myles. "Is there anything else I can do for you? I could come back…"

"No," said Elliot quickly. "Everything's fine, isn't it, Hester?"

Myles looked a bit surprised.

"I'm coping perfectly well, dear," said Hester. "And Elliot and the twins keep me company. Why don't you give me a ring sometime? I'd like that."

Myles smiled at her. "Of course I will." He jotted down Hester's number and Robert's number in New Zealand.

Elliot was anxious to get Myles away from Hester's as soon as possible. "I'll walk back with you," he told him. "It's nearly tea time."

He breathed a sigh of relief as they left. It had been a close thing but he'd got away with it – this time.

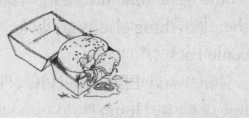

Chapter 12

Denzil
Something's Wrong With Hester!

Denzil had watched the sneezing man arrive through the fence, so his sixth sense had told him to keep out of the way. He hadn't actually needed Kai to come out and explain. *But it was pretty good of her*, he thought. *She obviously didn't realize that a streetwise dog like me soon picks up on what's what.*

He watched her and Abbie leave on their bikes just after Elliot and the sneezing man. *I hope they bring Sam with them again next time*, he thought.

Then Hester came out to give him the

dog food that Elliot had brought him. But she didn't seem quite right. She seemed distant somehow.

"What's the matter, Hester?" he barked. But of course she couldn't understand him.

Suddenly, she fell right to the ground in front of him. Denzil jumped back as the bowl of food crashed beside him.

Hester didn't get up. She just laid there on the cold ground and her body was twitching.

Denzil rushed to lick her face. Then he tried to rouse her with his nose. She didn't stir. "Hester! Hester!" he barked. "Wake up. Please get up." Nothing made any difference.

There was only one thing he could do. He'd have to get Elliot.

Elliot's scent was still fresh. *Here goes the bloodhound bit of me again*, he thought, as he raced along after him. *Good job I've got some greyhound in me too*.

He caught up with him just a couple of streets away. "Elliot!" he barked. "Elliot!"

Elliot turned round. He didn't look pleased to see Denzil at all. But there was no time to worry about that, he had to get him back to help Hester.

The sneezing man had gone all red again but he didn't start sneezing. "Where did that dog come from?" he shouted at Elliot.

Denzil barked impatiently at him. This was no time for arguing.

He jumped up and tugged on Elliot's coat sleeve. Then he ran a little way in the direction of Hester's and then back to Elliot. He repeated this a couple of times.

Elliot got the message. "There must be

something wrong with Hester," he cried. "I've got to go back."

Denzil raced ahead with Elliot and the sneezing man following. He led them straight into the garden and was relieved to find Hester sitting up. She looked a bit dazed.

Thank goodness, thought Denzil, and ran to lick her face.

"Get that dog away from her," shouted the sneezing man.

What a cheek! thought Denzil, as Elliot pulled him away and the man bent down himself to look at Hester.

"I think it was just a fit," she told him shakily. "I haven't had one for ages but I must admit, I don't always remember to take my tablets lately."

"Well, I think you should be checked out by your doctor," he said, helping her to her feet.

He turned on Elliot. "So that's why you

didn't want me to come back – you've been hiding your dog here, haven't you?"

Elliot nodded miserably. "But Denzil doesn't affect you here. I'm not doing any harm."

"You disobeyed your mother and me," said the sneezing man. "Just how long did you think you could keep it a secret? You must have known we'd find out eventually."

Then Hester spoke up. "Denzil actually arrived on his own and Elliot found him here," she said. "I'm happy to let the dog stay and Elliot takes care of him. He and the twins have been such a help to me."

"Yes, well that's not the point," said the man, leading her towards the house. Elliot followed them in and Denzil jumped up to look in the window.

The man had taken Hester into the sitting room and was looking round at the dust and cobwebs and the piles of stuff everywhere. "Oh dear, you're just not coping, are you, Hester? You really shouldn't be living here alone, especially as you're forgetting to take your tablets."

He pushed some papers aside and sat her down gently on the settee. "Don't you think you'd be better looked after in an old people's home?"

"She can't go into a home," cried Elliot.

Denzil was equally horrified. *No, she can't go into a home,* he thought. *Not an old lady like her. She couldn't possibly cope with living in one of those tiny kennels with just a bowl of food and water twice a day. Or with being turned out into a freezing cold run every morning.*

Denzil knew only too well what it was like. *And those baskets are much too small for her to sleep in,* he thought.

Chapter 13

Elliot
A Plan

Back at the flat that evening, while Myles was reading in the bedroom, Elliot complained bitterly to his mother. "Myles is ruining everything," he cried.

"No he's not, he's doing what's right," said Mum. "From what he told me, I have to agree with him that Hester would be better off in a home."

"But she doesn't want to go into a home," said Elliot. "She likes living there – and she likes having Denzil there too."

"You mustn't be selfish," said Mum.

"Hester needs help."

"But we were helping her," argued Elliot. "Before Myles interfered. You can't make her go into a home."

"It's not up to us," said Mum. "Myles has phoned Hester's son in New Zealand and he's coming over to sort his mother out."

She made it plain that she didn't want to discuss it any more. She'd been furious with Elliot for disobeying her about Denzil, and Myles had warned him not to upset her any more. The baby was due very soon.

At least Mum didn't try to stop Elliot from visiting Denzil and Hester. She even went with him a couple of times to see Hester herself.

Elliot continued to go every day and Mum sometimes sent a pie or a home-made cake for the old lady. Myles was busy working overtime at the bookshop, as they were stocktaking, but he phoned Hester regularly.

Elliot had come up with a plan. He eagerly explained it to Abbie and Kai. "If we can get Hester's house clean and tidy before her son comes from New Zealand, then he'll see she can cope on her own – at least with our help."

"Yes, and if we remind her to take her tablets every day," said Abbie. "She might not have any more fits."

Hester was in full agreement with all this.

The three children worked very hard. It was a large house and they cleaned, polished, vacuumed, tidied and washed floors and curtains. And Elliot still found time to feed and walk Denzil.

"I'm sure it's going to work," said Kai. "Hester's son is bound to be impressed."

"Robert's arriving on Saturday," Hester told them. "He phoned me this morning."

"That's great," said Elliot. "Myles will be working in the bookshop this Saturday.

So we'll get to him first." Things were looking hopeful.

But on Friday evening, when Elliot got home, a tall dark-haired man was sitting on the sofa with Myles. "This is Robert, Hester's son," Myles told Elliot.

"What? But you're not coming till tomorrow – you told Hester."

"I told Hester I would be going to see her tomorrow," said Robert. "But Myles wanted a word with me first."

Elliot turned on Myles. He was sick of his interfering. "How could you? You haven't given Hester a chance." He was never, ever going to speak to him again.

"Hey, don't get upset," said Robert. "I've been concerned for some time that my mother wasn't coping on her own. I'd got a good idea from her letters and phone calls."

"But she is coping now," cried Elliot. "With our help. You've got to go and look – the house is all cleaned and tidied up."

"Well that's good," said Robert. "It'll make it all the nicer for you to move in to."

"What?" Elliot looked round at his mother, who was smiling at him, and then at Myles and then back to Robert "But how can we…?"

"That's what Myles wanted to talk to me

about," Robert explained. "He suggested to me that you all move in with Hester to take care of her. There's plenty of room."

Myles's eyes glinted behind his glasses. "We didn't want to tell you in case it didn't work out," he told Elliot, with a big grin. "You'll have to help out of course – your mother will be busy with the new baby. But then you've been doing that already. And you'll have your own room there."

"Hester only really needs keeping an eye on at the moment," said Mum. "And later, when she needs more care, the baby will be older and I am a trained nurse so I'll be able to manage."

Elliot couldn't believe it. "But Hester—"

"—has already agreed," said Robert. "I've just spoken to her on the phone, while you were walking home. She's over the moon with the idea."

Elliot's mind was whirring – they'd be living in a house – with a garden – just like he'd always wanted. Myles had fixed it. But with Myles there…

"Oh no, what about Denzil?"

Myles came over to him and put his hand on his shoulder. "He can stay," he told him softly.

"But your allergy."

"He only affects me if he's indoors with me," said Myles. "Where the air is concentrated. As long as he stays outside in the fresh air, and I don't get too close, I'm OK. You must have noticed, I didn't sneeze once when I was in Hester's garden."

"Yes! And Denzil prefers to be outside," cried Elliot. "He won't be any trouble – I promise."

"He's a bright dog," said Myles. "Amazing how he came to get you when Hester was in trouble."

Elliot couldn't believe it. He didn't stop to think about it, he threw his arms round Myles's neck and hugged him. Then he hugged his mother and then Robert.

Robert laughed in surprise.

"I can't wait to tell Denzil tomorrow," said Elliot.

Chapter 14

Denzil
Something's Going On

Denzil wondered what was happening. Hester had brought a strange man called Robert out to see him first thing in the morning. She seemed to like him a lot.

I guess he must be all right, if Hester likes him, Denzil thought to himself, and he'd allowed Robert to stroke him. As soon as he'd gone back inside, Denzil had settled down to finish off last night's hamburger.

Then Elliot had opened the back gate. "Denzil. Guess what?"

But the sneezing man and the lady with the big tummy were with him too. The man grabbed Elliot's arm and pulled him back.

"Come and talk to Hester first," he said. "It's only polite."

"I'll be back in a minute," Elliot called to Denzil. "I've got something to tell you."

Denzil was just wondering what it could be when Abbie and Kai came round the back with Sam.

They left Sam in the garden with Denzil, then went into the house carrying some clean curtains.

"Something's going on," said Denzil.

"Everything seems fine to me," said Sam.

"Yes, well you haven't got razor sharp senses like me," said Denzil. "You've never been a dog of the road and had to fend for yourself. I've learned to be suspicious – always."

"Oh, come on…"

But Denzil wasn't listening. He trotted over to the house and stood up on his large back feet to look in the sitting-room window.

"Abbie and Kai are hanging up the curtains," he told Sam. "But the others are all talking."

"So? Humans do a lot of talking."

"So – I don't know – they all seem excited."

Sam jumped up to join him and peered in too. "Well, that's good, isn't it?"

"Not necessarily good for us," said Denzil. He tilted his head and strained his ears to hear what they were saying.

"I thought that you could have the bedroom at the back, Elliot," said Hester. "It overlooks the garden."

Bedroom? thought Denzil. *That's where humans sleep.*

"And you and Myles can have the big front room," Hester said to the lady with the big tummy. "And the small room next to it will be just right for the baby."

"What baby?" asked Denzil.

"I don't know," said Sam. "What's a baby anyway?"

"It's a human puppy," said Denzil.

Now Robert was speaking to them. "Mother and I won't be charging you any rent for living here, in return for looking after everything," he said. "That will give you a chance to save some money. Then, when you've got enough for a deposit, you might be able to get a loan and buy the house from us – eventually."

"Oh that's just wonderful," cried the lady with the big tummy. She put her arms round Hester. "Thank you, my dear. You won't have to worry about a thing – I promise you, you'll be taken very good care of."

"I don't believe it! They're moving in here," said Denzil. "They're putting Hester in a home to be taken care of and moving in themselves. And Hester seems to have agreed!"

"Why?" asked Sam.

"I don't know everything," said Denzil irritably.

Then Abbie and Kai said goodbye to everyone and came outside to get Sam.

"Well, it looks like my family's not moving in here anyway," said Sam. He jumped down to join the twins.

Denzil nodded and watched him trot off with them. *What's going to happen now?* he thought. He knew the sneezing man didn't like him anywhere near him. And the man had even told Elliot to get him away from Hester when she'd fallen. If he was moving in, then what...?

Elliot was talking now so Denzil cocked his head the other way to hear better. "And it's all due to Denzil," said Elliot.

He was getting the blame for something. *What have I done?* he wondered. *And why would Elliot blame me? I thought he loved me.*

Everyone was nodding in agreement but then the excitement appeared to be too much for the lady with the big tummy. She suddenly clutched her stomach and started groaning.

"The baby's coming," she cried.

Where? Denzil looked around him.

The sneezing man grabbed hold of the lady. "Come on, we'd better get you straight off to St Anthony's."

Is he taking her off to a home too? Maybe he's cross with her because she's making a fuss.

Denzil jumped down and ran round the side just in time to see them come out of the front.

"I'll drive you there," said Robert, opening a car door.

The sneezing man helped the lady inside then shouted at Elliot to hurry up.

Denzil was worried. He barked at Elliot to come and tell him what was happening.

"I must just tell Denzil about his home," said Elliot.

"There's no time," said the sneezing man. "Get into the car. We'll sort Denzil out later."

Oh no he won't! thought Denzil. *I'm not waiting around to be sent back to the home. I'm off.*

He briefly considered taking Hester with him too but he realized that an old lady like her couldn't possibly cope with life on the road. So he reluctantly left her behind as he plodded off down the street.

He'd been right all along – you could only trust yourself. "Why didn't I learn my lesson the first time Elliot let me down?" he asked himself. "Well, I'll make sure he never finds me again."

He turned into the park and stopped to check a couple of bushes for new smells. Then he had a drink from the pond. At least it wasn't frozen over and it tasted good. The water that humans gave you just didn't taste the same.

He sniffed the fresh air. "This is the life," he said. "Freedom. My own boss – no one to worry about except myself. King of the road again." This was how he really wanted to be.

He paused for a moment. If this was how he really wanted to be, then why did he feel so miserable?

Chapter 15

Elliot
Where's Denzil?

The baby – Bethany Jane – was finally born at six o'clock the following morning. And she didn't look a bit like a miniature Myles. In fact they said she had Elliot's nose.

Elliot was exhausted. He'd been up all night – they all had. The strange thing was, Mum didn't look tired at all now, sitting up holding Bethany.

But Myles insisted that she should rest now. "I'll take Elliot home and get us both some breakfast," he told her. Then he went off to call a taxi.

Elliot kissed his mother, and then Bethany. Bethany was really cute. He was surprised – he hadn't expected to actually *like* the baby.

Elliot felt very happy as they left the hospital, everything had worked out so well. It had been snowing again in the night and everywhere was covered with a fresh, white blanket. It seemed almost magical.

"Can we go and tell Denzil about us moving in and him staying too?" he asked Myles, as the taxi drew up.

Myles laughed as he opened the door. "All right. But he is only a dog, you know. He can't understand you."

Elliot didn't bother to argue. He *knew* Denzil understood him.

The taxi dropped them outside Hester's and Elliot rushed straight round to the back garden. "Denzil! Denzil. Guess what?" But there was no sign of the scruffy dog in the garden or the shed.

"Maybe he's gone out to get himself something to eat," said Elliot. Then Myles and Hester came out to see him.

"I'm sorry, Elliot," said Hester. "But Denzil left just after you yesterday and he hasn't been back."

"But that was ages ago," cried Elliot. "Something must have happened to him. I've got to find him."

"But, Elliot, we've had no sleep," started Myles.

"I don't care – and you don't have to come." He was already at the gate now.

"No, wait," said Myles. "I'll help you."

Elliot was surprised but very glad of the support.

They went out into the street together. "He's been gone some time," said Myles. "He could be anywhere."

"He might be lying injured somewhere," said Elliot. He couldn't bear the thought of the poor dog hurt and alone.

They started checking round the parked cars and over walls and fences into people's front gardens. There was no sign of the scruffy dog in any of the nearby streets.

"If only it hadn't snowed again," said Elliot. "We could have followed his footprints."

Then they checked round the hamburger restaurant and the back of the local shops but he wasn't there either.

"Where else did he like to go?" asked Myles.

"He liked the park," said Elliot.

So they made their way towards the park, calling him all the time.

They searched under bushes, behind trees and asked everyone they met if they'd seen him, but no one had. There was no shortage of doggy footprints in the park but, of course, any of the larger ones could have been Denzil's.

It was really cold and they stamped their

feet to keep themselves warm. Myles sniffed the air and grinned. "Maybe I'll start sneezing – then we'll know we're close."

"But it doesn't affect you in the open air," said Elliot. He knew Myles was attempting to cheer him up with his joke but he couldn't even smile.

"I do actually like dogs," Myles told him, as they investigated yet another bush. "It's just this allergy – and there aren't many places you can keep a dog outside. Plus most dogs wouldn't want to live outside – it wouldn't be kind."

"No, Denzil's different," said Elliot. "He's just – perfect…" He almost choked on the last word.

Myles put his arm round his shoulders. "Come on, we haven't looked over here yet."

They moved off to search yet more bushes and trees.

It was almost lunchtime when Myles said, "I'm sorry, Elliot, but I've got to go back to the hospital this afternoon. And I really do think we need something hot to eat and drink."

"That's all right, you go," said Elliot. He'd been surprised and grateful that Myles had helped him at all. "Mum will want to see you and I know you'll want to be with Bethany."

He looked round at the big expanse of white. It looked hopeless – Denzil could be anywhere – even miles away by now. He felt so alone. Mum had the baby now and Myles was bound to be more interested in his own daughter than him. And he – Elliot – didn't have Denzil any more.

"Look, Bethany isn't going to be more important than you," said Myles, as if he knew what he was thinking. "I know I'm not your real dad and I know I don't always get things right. But I do think of you as my son and we're mates as well, right? After all, you're my right-hand man for putting up shelves."

Elliot nodded. Myles was really trying.

"I'll stay another half an hour if you like," Myles offered.

"Thanks." Elliot managed a smile. "Denzil's obviously not in the park, so we might as well look somewhere else."

They made their way towards the park gates.

Chapter 12

Denzil

"I love you, Denzil."

Denzil watched Elliot and the sneezing man from inside his bush. *Why are they bothering to look for me?* he wondered. *Are they really that keen to get me back in the home? The man's obsessed! He's obviously taken the lady with the big tummy to one as she's not with them now.*

He was cold and miserable. Even the hamburgers he'd collected last night hadn't cheered him up. "I was fine before I got tangled up with humans," he growled to himself. "Never, ever again."

At least it looked as if they were going now. Denzil shrank back further into the darkness of his bush as they walked past.

Then the sneezing man kicked something in the snow and stooped to pick it up. "Look at this," he said to Elliot. "A hamburger carton. It's disgraceful the way people drop litter."

He's always moaning, thought Denzil. *How am I supposed to get them in the litter bin?*

"And here's another one," said the sneezing man, gathering it up. "And another. Have people actually been having a picnic in the snow?"

"Hamburgers!" cried Elliot, taking the carton from him.

"Er – yes, Elliot." The sneezing man looked puzzled.

"Don't you see?" cried Elliot. "Hamburgers – Denzil – he loves them. Look, there's even teeth marks on this carton. He's got to be here somewhere."

Denzil tried to back out of the bush but there was a big branch behind him, stopping him. Then Elliot was on his hands and knees in the snow, peering into the bush.

"Denzil! You're here." Elliot parted the branches and tried to crawl in to him.

The sneezing man stopped him. "Better get him to come out," he said. "It's dangerous to make an animal feel trapped. I read it in one of my books."

Feel trapped? thought Denzil. *That's exactly what he's trying to do – trap me in a home.*

"Denzil, please come out," Elliot coaxed. "Why did you run away? Did you think I'd left you? I wouldn't have – I just didn't get a chance to tell you everything."

Denzil didn't move. *You're not fooling me again,* he thought.

"And guess what?" said Elliot. "You don't make Myles sneeze when you're outside."

Me? thought Denzil. *What's it got to do with me? Why do I always get the blame?*

"Oh, come on, Denzil," Elliot pleaded.

"We're all going to be together now. You, me, Hester, Myles, Mum and the new baby – one big family. Myles has fixed it. We're never going to be parted again – not ever. I promise you."

The sneezing man bent down towards him, although he seemed to be keeping his distance. "I'll even give you one of my home-made hamburgers," he told him.

Denzil wasn't sure he trusted him – even with the offer of hamburgers. But then he looked into Elliot's eyes. You could tell a lot by people's eyes. Elliot looked sincere, loving. *Real soulful eyes*, he thought.

He decided to venture out slowly.

Elliot immediately hugged him, then he brushed some snow off his face, then hugged him again. "Oh, I love you, Denzil."

Even the sneezing man was smiling. Denzil didn't understand quite what was going on but he now knew for certain the most important thing – that Elliot loved him. Somehow that was all that mattered and he didn't mind who came to live with them – even this baby everyone kept talking about – just as long as he was with Elliot.

"Come on, boy," said Elliot, and Denzil followed him, boy and dog happily running and jumping through the snow together.

"You know what, Denzil?" Elliot called to him. "You really are the best dog in the world."